Spider Web

Tracy Kompelien

Illustrated by Anne Haberstroh

Consulting Editor, Diane Craig, M.A./Reading Specialist

ABDO
Publishing Company

Published by ABDO Publishing Company, 4940 Viking Drive, Edina, Minnesota 55435.

Printed in the United States.

Credits
Edited by: Pam Price
Curriculum Coordinator: Nancy Tuminelly
Cover and Interior Design and Production: Mighty Media
Photo Credits: ShutterStock

Library of Congress Cataloging-in-Publication Data

Kompelien, Tracy, 1975-
    Spider web / Tracy Kompelien; illustrated by Anne Haberstroh.
        p. cm. -- (Fact & fiction. Critter chronicles)
    Summary: Spencer the spider's beautiful webs always unravel, but he is determined to use his creativity to make a web that will last. Alternating pages provide facts about spiders and their webs.
        ISBN 10 1-59928-474-X (hardcover)
        ISBN 10 1-59928-475-8 (paperback)

        ISBN 13 978-1-59928-474-3 (hardcover)
        ISBN 13 978-1-59928-475-0 (paperback)
        [1. Determination (Personality trait)--Fiction. 2. Spider webs--Fiction. 3. Spiders--Fiction.]
    I. Haberstroh, Anne, ill. II. Title. III. Series.)

    PZ7.K83497Spi 2007
    [E]--dc22
                                                                                    2006005706

SandCastle Level: Fluent

SandCastle™ books are created by a professional team of educators, reading specialists, and content developers around five essential components—phonemic awareness, phonics, vocabulary, text comprehension, and fluency—to assist young readers as they develop reading skills and strategies and increase their general knowledge. All books are written, reviewed, and leveled for guided reading, early reading intervention, and Accelerated Reader® programs for use in shared, guided, and independent reading and writing activities to support a balanced approach to literacy instruction. The SandCastle™ series has four levels that correspond to early literacy development. The levels help teachers and parents select appropriate books for young readers.

Emerging Readers	**Beginning Readers**	**Transitional Readers**	**Fluent Readers**
(no flags)	(1 flag)	(2 flags)	(3 flags)

These levels are meant only as a guide. All levels are subject to change.

FACT & FICTION

This series provides early fluent readers the opportunity to develop reading comprehension strategies and increase fluency. These books are appropriate for guided, shared, and independent reading.

FACT The left-hand pages incorporate realistic photographs to enhance readers' understanding of informational text.

Fiction The right-hand pages engage readers with an entertaining, narrative story that is supported by whimsical illustrations.

The Fact and Fiction pages can be read separately to improve comprehension through questioning, predicting, making inferences, and summarizing. They can also be read side-by-side, in spreads, which encourages students to explore and examine different writing styles.

FACT OR Fiction? This fun quiz helps reinforce students' understanding of what is real and not real.

SPEED READ The text-only version of each section includes word-count rulers for fluency practice and assessment.

GLOSSARY Higher-level vocabulary and concepts are defined in the glossary.

SandCastle™ would like to hear from you.

Tell us your stories about reading this book. What was your favorite page? Was there something hard that you needed help with? Share the ups and downs of learning to read. To get posted on the ABDO Publishing Company Web site, send us an e-mail at:

sandcastle@abdopublishing.com

The hair and claws on spiders' legs allow them to cling to their webs. The oils on their bodies keep them from sticking to their own webs.

"Ouch!" Spencer screams as he hits the hard floor. Spencer worked on his web all day, only for it to break as he was finishing. "Not again," he mumbles as he makes his way back up the wall.

Spiders make their webs from several different kinds of spider silk. They make the framework first, then fill it in.

Spencer loves to make beautiful webs. He is the most creative spider in the basement. Unfortunately, he has trouble making a web that lasts.

Spiders are recyclers. They eat their old
webs to make more silk for new webs.

"Spencer is working so hard on his web. Doesn't he know Tuesday is cleaning day?" the other spiders say.

9

Vibrations on the web let a spider know it
has caught an insect.

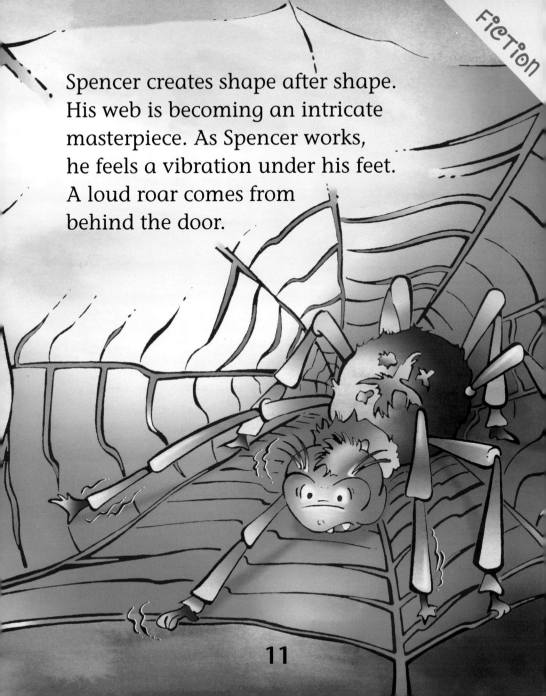

Spencer creates shape after shape. His web is becoming an intricate masterpiece. As Spencer works, he feels a vibration under his feet. A loud roar comes from behind the door.

11

A spider uses from 22 to 66 yards of silk to make a web. It takes a spider about three hours to spin a web.

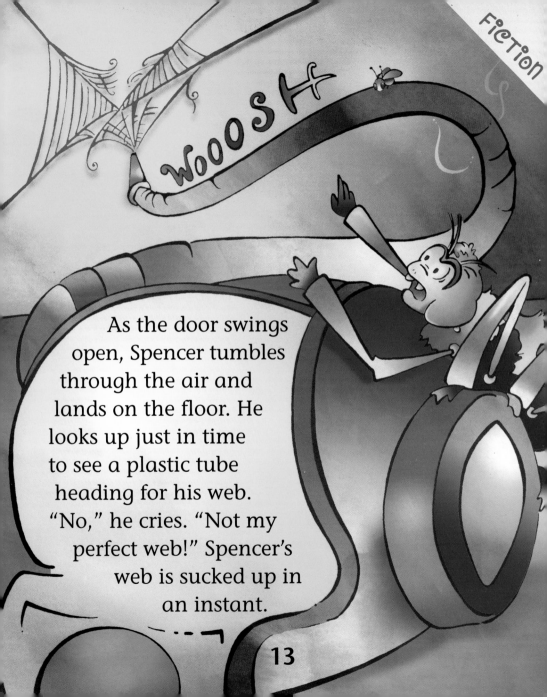

WOOOSH

As the door swings open, Spencer tumbles through the air and lands on the floor. He looks up just in time to see a plastic tube heading for his web. "No," he cries. "Not my perfect web!" Spencer's web is sucked up in an instant.

Over time, spiders have adapted to live in many habitats. They can be found on the ground, in trees and plants, in caves, and even on the water.

Spencer is starting to think that
he will never make a durable web.
"I will have to be more creative
than ever before," Spencer decides.
For his next attempt, he finds a
new spot under the furnace. The
other spiders are in awe of
Spencer's determination.

15

Spider silk is very elastic and strong. Some spider silks are stronger than a strand of steel that is the same diameter.

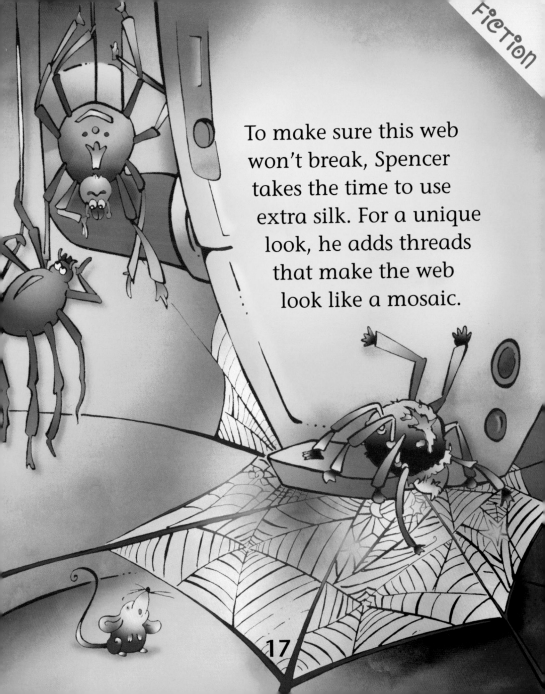

To make sure this web won't break, Spencer takes the time to use extra silk. For a unique look, he adds threads that make the web look like a mosaic.

17

There are about 35,000 known species of spiders.

Once the web is finished,
Spencer invites all of the basement
spiders over. They are hesitant, but
the web holds the entire party! The
spiders all congratulate Spencer on
his beautiful and sturdy web.

19

Read each statement below. Then decide whether it's from the FACT section or the FICTION section!

  1. Spiders can talk.

  2. Spiders live in many places.

  3. Spider silk is strong.

 4. Spiders have parties.

The hair and claws on spiders' legs allow them to cling to their webs. The oils on their bodies keep them from sticking to their own webs.

Spiders make their webs from several different kinds of spider silk. They make the framework first, then fill it in.

Spiders are recyclers. They eat their old webs to make more silk for new webs.

Vibrations on the web let a spider know it has caught an insect.

A spider uses from 22 to 66 yards of silk to make a web. It takes a spider about three hours to spin a web.

Over time, spiders have adapted to live in many habitats. They can be found on the ground, in trees and plants, in caves, and even on the water.

Spider silk is very elastic and strong. Some spider silks are stronger than a strand of steel that is the same diameter.

There are about 35,000 known species of spiders.

"Ouch!" Spencer screams as he hits the hard 8
floor. Spencer worked on his web all day, only for 18
it to break as he was finishing. "Not again," he 28
mumbles as he makes his way back up the wall. 38

Spencer loves to make beautiful webs. He is 46
the most creative spider in the basement. 53
Unfortunately, he has trouble making a web 60
that lasts. 62

"Spencer is working so hard on his web. Doesn't 71
he know Tuesday is cleaning day?" the other 79
spiders say. 81

Spencer creates shape after shape. His web is 89
becoming an intricate masterpiece. As Spencer 95
works, he feels a vibration under his feet. A loud 105
roar comes from behind the door. 111

As the door swings open, Spencer tumbles 118
through the air and lands on the floor. He looks 128
up just in time to see a plastic tube heading for 139

his web. "No," he cries. "Not my perfect web!" 148
Spencer's web is sucked up in an instant. 156

Spencer is starting to think that he will never 165
make a durable web. "I will have to be more 175
creative than ever before," Spencer decides. For his 183
next attempt, he finds a new spot under the 192
furnace. The other spiders are in awe of Spencer's 201
determination. 202

To make sure this web won't break, Spencer takes 211
the time to use extra silk. For a unique look, he 222
adds threads that make the web look like a mosaic. 232

Once the web is finished, Spencer invites all of the 242
basement spiders over. They are hesitant, but the web 251
holds the entire party! The spiders all congratulate 259
Spencer on his beautiful and sturdy web. 266

GLOSSARY

creative. having the ability to make something original

determined. having made a firm decision about something

durable. long lasting and able to withstand wear

habitat. the area or environment where a person or thing usually lives

intricate. having parts that are arranged in a complex or elaborate manner

mosaic. a decorative design made up of many small parts

unique. the only one of its kind

vibration. the act of moving rapidly back and forth

To see a complete list of SandCastle™ books and other nonfiction titles from ABDO Publishing Company, visit www.abdopublishing.com or contact us at: 4940 Viking Drive, Edina, Minnesota 55435 • 1-800-800-1312 • fax: 1-952-831-1632